D0255768

ROTHERHAM LIBRARY & INFORMATION SERVICE

This book must be returned by the date specified at the time of issue as
the DATE DUE FOR RETURN.
The loan may be extended (personally, by post, telephone or online) for
a further period if the book is not required by another reader, by quoting
the above number / author / title.

Enquiries: 01709 336774

www.rotherham.gov.uk/libraries

ISBN 978 1 4052 5775 6

1 3 5 7 9 10 8 6 4 2

Printed in Italy

48547/1

Egmont is passionate about helping to preserve the world's remaining ancient forests.
We only use paper from legal and sustainable forest sources.

This book is made from paper certified by the Forestry Stewardship Council (FSC),
an organisation dedicated to promoting responsible management of forest resources.
For more information on the FSC, please visit www.fsc.org. To learn more about
Egmont's sustainable paper policy, please visit www.egmont.co.uk/ethical

Winnie-the-Pooh
Pooh's Snowy Day

EGMONT

One morning Pooh wasn't doing very much, so he thought he would go and visit Piglet. But when he got to Piglet's house, Piglet wasn't there. Bother, thought Pooh to himself, and he decided to go back home.

When Pooh got back to his own house, he
found Piglet sitting in his best armchair.
For a moment he wondered whose house he was in.

"Hello Piglet," he said. "I thought you were out."

"No," said Piglet. "It's you who were out, Pooh!"

When they had had a little something to eat, Pooh and Piglet decided to visit Eeyore. On the way they sang a special outdoor song that Pooh had written:

"The more it snows, Tiddley Pom!" it went.

By this time Pooh and Piglet were close to where Eeyore lived.

"I've been thinking," said Pooh. "Eeyore's place is very gloomy. Why don't we build him a new house?"

"I saw a heap of sticks on the other side of the wood," said Piglet, helpfully.

"Let's go and fetch them," said Pooh, "and build a house here."

A little bit later, Christopher Robin was just about to go outside when who should arrive at his front door but Eeyore.

"Hello Christopher Robin," said Eeyore. "I don't suppose you've seen my house anywhere, have you?"

"Your house?" said Christopher Robin.

"It gets very cold on my side of the forest,"
explained Eeyore. "So I built myself a little
house to keep warm in, and I went back there this
morning, and IT'S GONE!"

"Oh, Eeyore," said Christopher Robin.

Eyore and Christopher Robin set off together to look for Eeyore's little house.

"There!" said Eeyore, "You see. Not a stick of it left!"

But Christopher Robin wasn't listening. In the distance he could hear ... what was it?

Christopher Robin moved closer to where
the strange sound was coming from. It sounded
like two voices singing–first a gruff one and then
a higher, squeakier one.

"It's Pooh and Piglet!" said Christopher Robin.

Sure enough, there were Pooh and Piglet coming toward them.

"There's Christopher Robin!" squeaked Piglet.

"He's over by the place where we found all those sticks!"

After Christopher Robin had given Pooh a hug, he told Pooh and Piglet about the sad story of Eeyore's lost house. And the more he talked, the more Pooh and Piglet's eyes seemed to get bigger and bigger.

"The fact is ..." said Pooh. "Well, the fact is ..."

"It's like this," said Piglet "... only WARMER."

"What's warmer?" asked Christopher Robin.

"The other side of the wood, where Eeyore's house is," said Piglet. "We'll show you," said Pooh.

So they went over to the other side of the forest, and sure enough there was Eeyore's house.

"It IS my house," said Eeyore. "And I built it where I said I did. The wind must have blown it here." And Eeyore happily settled down in his new house.

Pooh, Piglet and Christopher Robin went back home to lunch, and on the way Pooh and Piglet told him about the Awful Mistake they had made. Christopher Robin just laughed, and they all sang Pooh's song all the way home.

Tiddley Pom! Tiddley Pom!

More Winnie-the-Pooh titles to enjoy!

Count down from 10 to 1
with these 3D busy bees

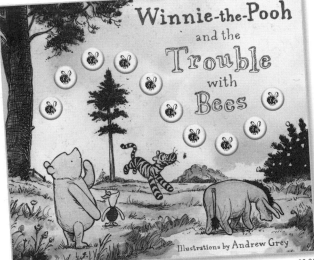

ISBN: 978 14052 5130 3

£9.99

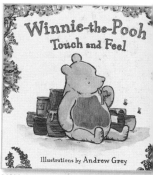

ISBN: 978 14052 5670 4

Tickle Pooh's fluffy
tummy and find the
sticky honey

Beautiful
buggy books...

Winnie
-the-
Pooh
Buggy Book

ISBN: 978 1405 2 5579 0
£4.99

Letters to open, a card to
read and surprise gifts too!

Winnie-the-Pooh
and the
Grand Christmas Surprise
Illustrations by Andrew Grey

With five special letters and press-out Christmas decorations!

ISBN: 978 1405 2 6067 1

£9.99

Tigger
Buggy
Book

ISBN: 978 1405 2 5580 6
£4.99

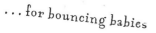

... for bouncing babies